SPACE DOG

Mini Grey

Alfred A. Knopf
New York

It's the year **3043** and, for as long as anyone can remember, on **HOME PLANET**

ASTRO

SPACE DOGS,

ANOTHER BIG ST
QUEST TO DISCOVER MILK & CREAM IN DISTANT GALAXIES

have been **SWORN**

CATS, and MOUSTRONAUTS

ENEMIES.

(After all, that's the way it has always been.)

But there's no time for that now, because . . .

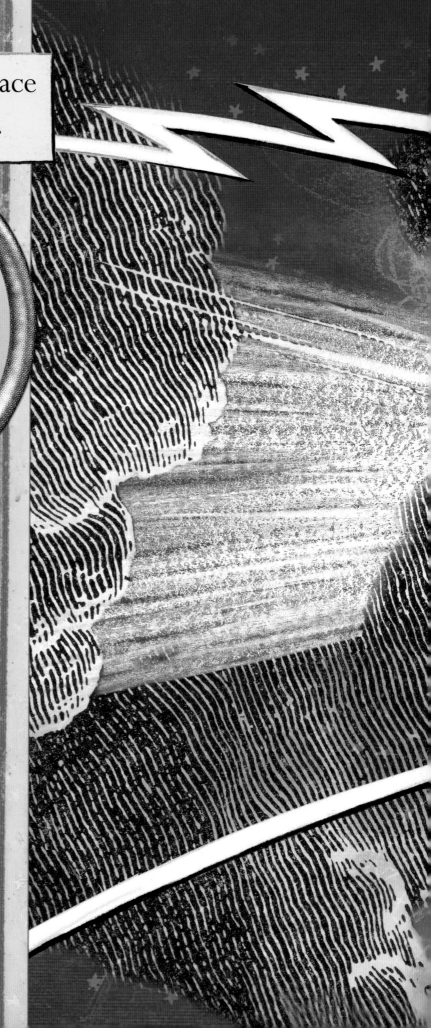

. . . in the vast deeps of space
a small ship is zooming.

At last,
Space Dog
is about
to go

HOME.

It has been a long mission
sorting out planetary problems
in the Dairy Quadrant.

It all started with distress calls from the Breakfast Cluster.

Space Dog—we need help! Our planet is suffering from a terrible dryness! All our milk lakes have dried up. We can't carry on like this.

Space Dog—we're awash with milk! Our homes are flooding— we haven't got much time.

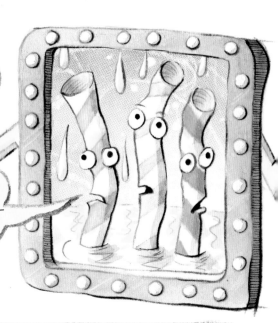

Sure enough, the atmosphere on Cornflake 5 was much too dry and crunchy . . .

. . . whereas nearby Bottleopolis was afloat with milk.

PINGOS

INSTANT SLOOP

JAM CLUSTERS

WING NUTS

MICRO DOTS

FROSTICLES

RICE-O

So dry! So dry!

Thundering milkswamps! I'd better hurry. . . .

Aaargh, so very dry!

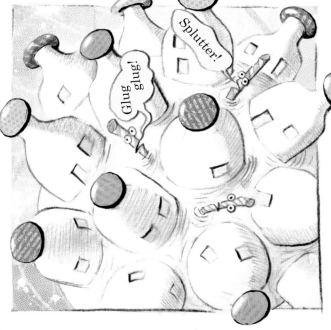

Glug glug!

Splutter!

It looked like a job for Space Dog.

SD

Things carried on . . .

with the evacuation of a Colossal Stink from Bath Time 37,

making contact with a Spaghetti Entity in the Pastaroid Belt, and rescuing the people of Niblet 12 from an escaped pet that had gone on the rampage.

Then there was just time to judge a hat competition . . .

. . . before Space Dog returned to his ship, the SS *Kennel*.

Time to go home.

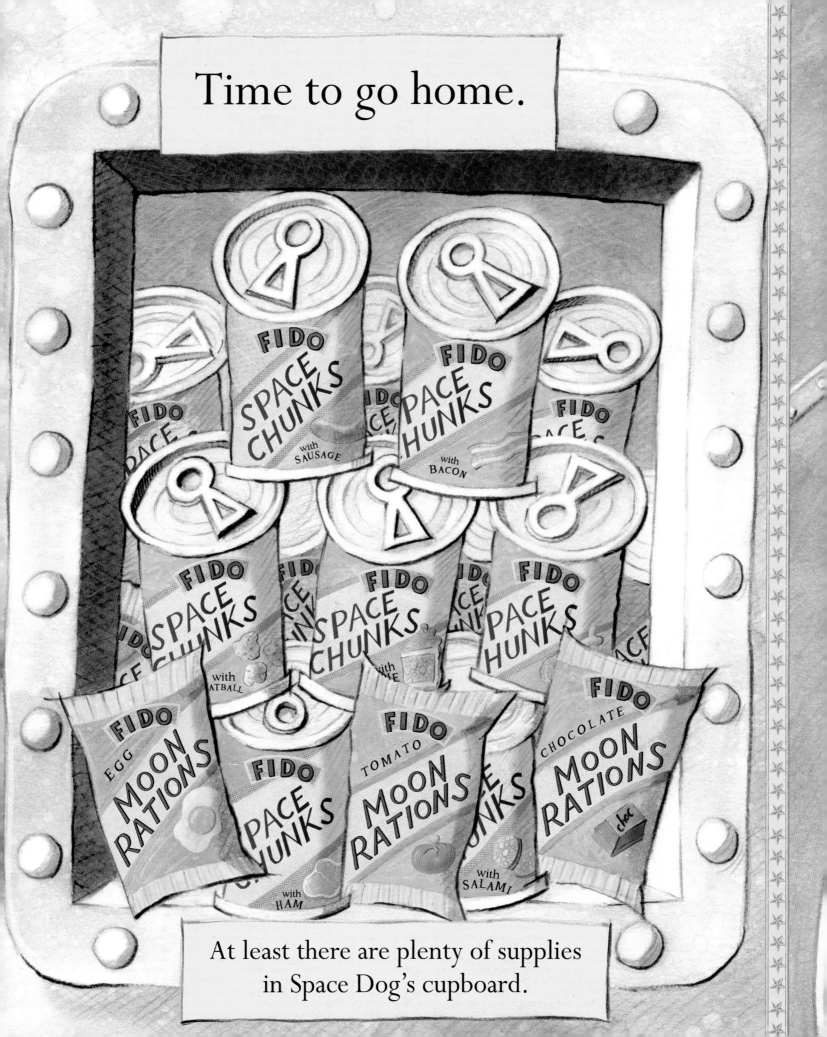

At least there are plenty of supplies
in Space Dog's cupboard.

On board his ship,
Space Dog has
his usual dinner,

* Sigh *

HOME SWEET HOME

No Place like Home

and then he plays
Dogopoly
on his own . . .

. . . before he sleeps in his bunk
and dreams of his Home Planet,
shining like a beautiful marble
in space.

HOME
PLANET

Meanwhile

somewhere not so far away in
the Dairy Quadrant, Astrocat is also
zooming in his saucer.

Mmmm. Destination: Cream!

Suddenly Space Dog is woken by a distress call
coming through on his Laser Display Screen.

The saucer is sinking too quickly to be rescued,
but Space Dog pulls out the occupant.

AN ASTROCAT!

"But Astrocats and Space Dogs are Sworn Enemies!" gulps Astrocat.

"But there's no time for that now!" says Space Dog.

Space Dog drags Astrocat out of the thick cream and takes him aboard his own ship.

Your saucer is lost—you'd better hitch a ride on the SS *Kennel*.

What in CakeSpace am I going to do with an **Astrocat** on board?

When Astrocat has dried off . . .

. . . it turns out he is surprisingly
good at playing Dogopoly,

and can also rustle up
a tasty little something
from Space Dog's
supplies.

Time for them
both to go home.

Space Dog and Astrocat
are just setting
the coordinates
when—
A DISTRESS
CALL!

SOMEBODY PLEASE HELP US—THEY'RE GONNA BLOW!

Great balls of pudding!
I had no idea that
Astrocats could cook!

A cry for help, Astrocat.

Well, we'd better answer
it, then, Space Dog.

Back on the ship,
Space Dog
is finally
setting
the controls
for

HOME

The UNKNOWN

when—

HOME
SWEET
HOME

HELP!

No
P

WHIFF
WHIFF

SOUVENIR OF EARTH

A distress call on the Laser Display Screen
Coming from this distinctly cheesy planet
They simply **have** to help.

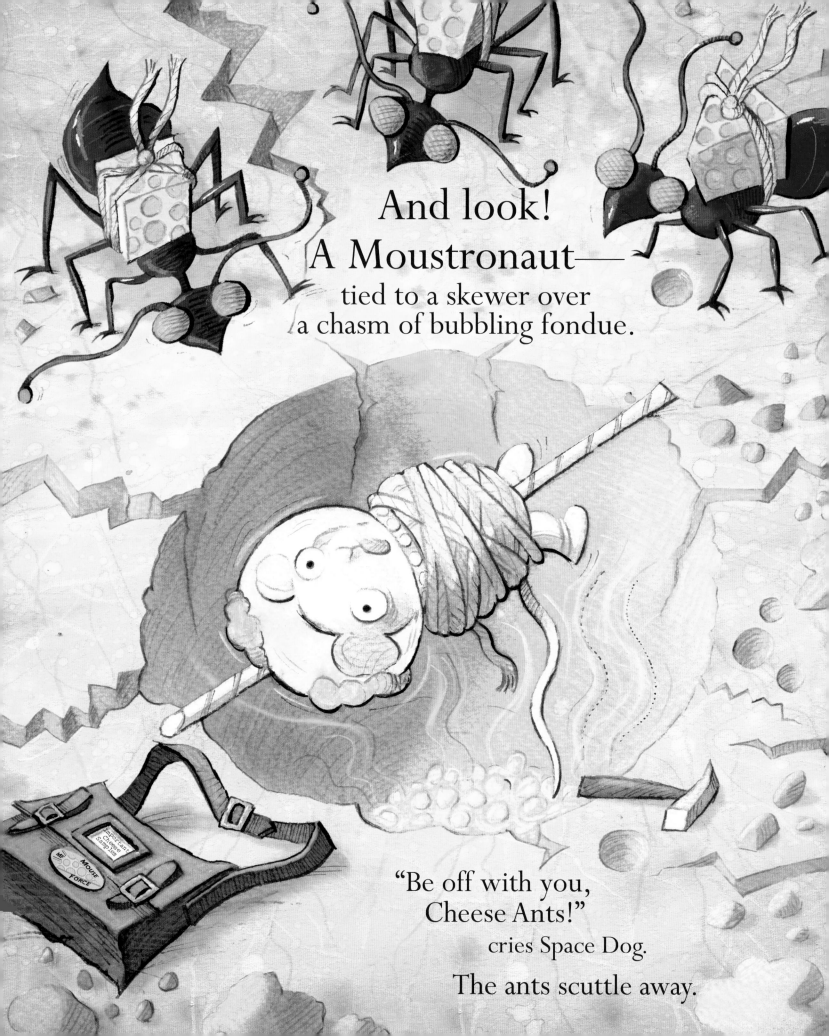

And look!
A Moustronaut—
tied to a skewer over
a chasm of bubbling fondue.

"Be off with you,
Cheese Ants!"
cries Space Dog.

The ants scuttle away.

"Grab my tail, Space Dog," says Astrocat,
   balancing precariously and untangling the rope.
   "BUT MOUSTRONAUTS AND ASTROCATS ARE SWORN ENEMIES!"
gasps the Moustronaut.
   "But there's no time
      for that now!"
         Astrocat replies.
   "MY SATCHEL!
         MY SATCHEL!"
screams the
      Moustronaut.

Astrocat grabs the satchel,
and, getting ready to run,
they turn round
      to see . . .

Her mandibles are dribbling and there's a hungry look in her compound eyes.

But then the Moustronaut has an idea.

She offers the Queen the cheese samples from her satchel—

rare samples from the farthest reaches of space— and bows respectfully.

Fromage

The Queen lowers her feelers.

THE CHEESE SAMPLES MUST HAVE BEEN WHAT SHE WANTED. SHE MUST BE A CHEESE COLLECTOR, TOO!

But this planet is full of holes and crumbling fast.

They dash to the ship and blast off just in time . . .

. . . as, with a lurching groan, the planet implodes.

On board Space Dog's ship, they scrape the cheesy goo off the Moustronaut, and Astrocat runs her a nice bath.

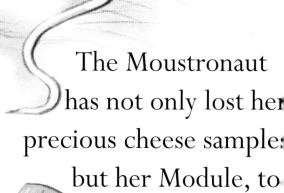

The Moustronaut has not only lost her precious cheese samples but her Module, too.

Very Important Cheese

"Cheer up, Moustronaut," says Astrocat.
"We need a quick-thinking mouse on our team.

Someone
with nimble fingers

and amazing
powers of sniff."

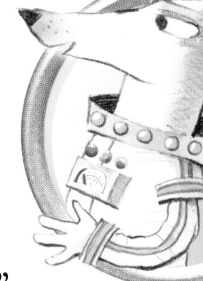

"Yes," says
Space Dog.

"Someone who is brave in
the face of giant insects,

and a third player
for Dogopoly.

Now we can go Home."

BACK TO...

HOME PLANET—WHERE SPACE DOGS, ASTROCATS, AND MOUSTRONAUTS CAN BE

ENEMIES FOREVER

Everyone is quiet for a moment.

"BUT THERE'S NO TIME FOR THAT NOW!" cries the Moustronaut. "THERE'S A WHOLE UNIVERSE OUT THERE— ONE WHERE SPACE DOGS, ASTROCATS, AND MOUSTRONAUTS CAN BE SWORN FRIENDS."

HOME

Near to the
Home button
on his control panel
is another one that
Space Dog hasn't
noticed before.

THE
UNKNOWN
ZONE

"Shall we?"
"OF COURSE!"
"Why not!"

And they set
controls for
THE

UNKNOWN
ZONE.

In the vast deeps of space,
a small ship is zooming.
Adventures could be
on the horizon,
or even just round
the corner.

But for now,
Space Dog, Astrocat, and
the Moustronaut are playing
Dogopoly before dinner.

Nobody is *completely* sure
of the exact rules . . .

. . . but it doesn't seem to matter.

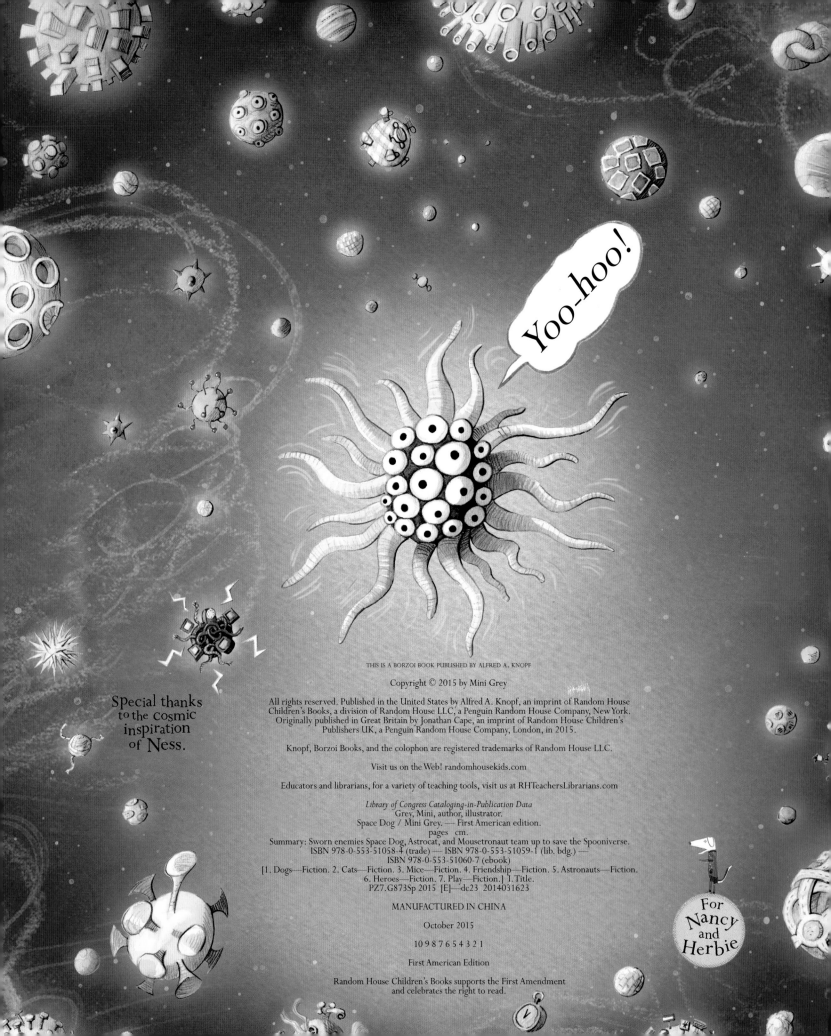

Yoo-hoo!

Special thanks
to the cosmic
inspiration
of Ness.

For
Nancy
and
Herbie

THIS IS A BORZOI BOOK PUBLISHED BY ALFRED A. KNOPF

Copyright © 2015 by Mini Grey

All rights reserved. Published in the United States by Alfred A. Knopf, an imprint of Random House
Children's Books, a division of Random House LLC, a Penguin Random House Company, New York.
Originally published in Great Britain by Jonathan Cape, an imprint of Random House Children's
Publishers UK, a Penguin Random House Company, London, in 2015.

Knopf, Borzoi Books, and the colophon are registered trademarks of Random House LLC.

Visit us on the Web! randomhousekids.com

Educators and librarians, for a variety of teaching tools, visit us at RHTeachersLibrarians.com

Library of Congress Cataloging-in-Publication Data
Grey, Mini, author, illustrator.
Space Dog / Mini Grey. — First American edition.
pages   cm.
Summary: Sworn enemies Space Dog, Astrocat, and Mousetronaut team up to save the Spooniverse.
ISBN 978-0-553-51058-4 (trade) — ISBN 978-0-553-51059-1 (lib. bdg.) —
ISBN 978-0-553-51060-7 (ebook)
[1. Dogs—Fiction. 2. Cats—Fiction. 3. Mice—Fiction. 4. Friendship—Fiction. 5. Astronauts—Fiction.
6. Heroes—Fiction. 7. Play—Fiction.] I. Title.
PZ7.G873Sp 2015 [E]—dc23 2014031623

MANUFACTURED IN CHINA

October 2015

10 9 8 7 6 5 4 3 2 1

First American Edition